About the Author

Audie Willert was born in the Philippines but grew up in NYC from the age of two. In 1977, he formed a punk rock band, the 2Timers with high school friends and convinced them to go to London where they got a singles' deal with Virgin Records. Audie graduated from Hunter College NYC with a B.A. in History in 1989. Stonybrook University New York with an M.A. in English 1991. The University of New South Wales, Sydney, with a graduate degree in Law 2001. He practiced as a criminal lawyer for Legal Aid Sydney for 12 years.

Audie studied Tae Kwon Do in NYC from the late master son for thirteen years and is a third degree blackbelt, teaching Tae Kwon Do in New York, Tokyo and Sydney. He currently teaches English at the College of Southern Nevada.in Las Vegas.

Henry

Audie Willert

Henry

Olympia Publishers
London

www.olympiapublishers.com
OLYMPIA PAPERBACK EDITION

A CIP catalogue record for this title is
available from the British Library.

ISBN: 978-1-80439-093-1

This is a work of fiction.
Names, characters, places and incidents originate from the writer's
imagination. Any resemblance to actual persons, living or dead, is
purely coincidental.

First Published in 2023

Olympia Publishers
Tallis House
2 Tallis Street
London
EC4Y 0AB

Printed in Great Britain

Dedication

This book is dedicated to Henry Willert, born in Dalhart Texas twenty-nine April 2013; died in Henderson NV, nineteen December 2019. More than a dog, more than a friend, the perfect being.

Acknowledgements

Thanks to my wife, Mary, for encouraging me and reading the endless rough drafts of *Henry*. Making sure the substance and purity of his spirit were captured on the pages.

CHAPTER 1

"Mom, you know my birthday's next month and the present you promised me," said the boy as he dried the dish his mother handed him.

"Oh, I haven't forgotten Billy," she replied, handing him another dish to dry.

"For the past year I've done all my chores, kept my room clean, and got all As and Bs on my report card."

"Yes, I know, and I'm very proud of you, you've kept your end of our contract; and I'm gonna keep mine, but why are you asking me this now? There's still another month to go till your birthday," she said, as she handed him another dish.

"Aw ma," he pleaded, "it's just that I haven't seen or heard you do anything about getting a puppy."

"Billy," she said seriously, "you know how busy I am at the hospital with all my patients and paperwork. We nurses work really hard, and on top of all that I've gotta take care of you, do the shopping, laundry, cleaning, pay our bills," as she stopped to look her son straight in the eyes. "I've made calls to several breeders during my lunch hours. I promised I'd get you a puppy for your twelfth birthday, now let's finish up with this dish washing; I wanna sit down and relax."

"But, mom, it's gotta be an Airedale puppy, and I know they're not easy to find" – he pleaded – "not just any puppy, but an Airedale."

"Yes I know, Billy," she replied, stopping what she was doing and looking softly in his eyes, feeling his anxiety. "I've spoken to a breeder in Texas and put a deposit on a male Airedale puppy, and he'll be here on your birthday, the twenty-ninth April; and I've already told her the name you've chosen for your pup, Henry. And she's already started calling him that. Happy now?" she said smiling.

"Really!" said Billy beaming, and giving his mom a big hug with a smile on his face. She put down the pan she was holding and wrapped her arms around her son. The two of them feeling the love flow from one another. He's almost as tall as me she thought; as she kissed him on the top of his head while giving him one last hug.

"Now let's finish up cleaning these pots and pans."

Although she'd heard him tell her dozens of times over the past year why he wanted an Airedale; she wanted to hear him again, to reassure herself he would be responsible enough to take care of a young puppy, which she knew from experience would be a handful with all the teething, training and cleaning.

"So why an Airedale?" she asked, "And why the name Henry?"

"AW, Mom, I've told you a thousand times already."

"Well, tell me again hon" – handing him the last pan to dry – "I love hearing your Airedale story."

"As I told you before, mom, an Airedale named Jake was the first dog to get the Victoria Cross for bravery by the British army in WWI, that's like our medal of honor. It was trench warfare and the British used Airedales to jump in and out of trenches and crawl under barbed wire to deliver messages on the battlefield. They needed a dog that was not too big and easily shot like a German Shepherd, but not too small as they had to be strong and fast; and Airedales turned out to be the best dogs as they were strong, brave, intelligent and easy to train. Jake was shot fourteen times by the Germans and with a broken leg still delivered his last message to a captain in the trenches, warning him the German army was about to attack, saving hundreds of lives before dying at his feet."

"I hope Henry doesn't have such a traumatic ending," said his mother seriously.

"And since Airedales are originally from England," he continued, "we read about Henry, the VIII, in class, and Airedales are called the king of terriers because they're the biggest, so it made sense to name my puppy after a king."

"Can't argue with that logic," said his mother, while thinking how smart her son was becoming.

CHAPTER 2

True to her word, Henry arrived by plane in a traveling crate on twenty-ninth April. The breeder loaded Henry and three of his litter mates on the flat bed of her pick-up truck in Dalhart Texas and drove them to Amarillo to fly to their new homes in different parts of the country. His mother had taken the day off to drive to the airport to pick Henry up while Billy was at school. After driving around parts of the airport she never even knew existed, she finally found the right loading dock, and parked her SUV in the loading bay, dwarfed by the big trucks receiving air freight from all over the country.

After giving the man at the loading dock her paperwork and ID, he returned a few minutes later and handed her a small crate with a puppy inside. Peering inside, she thought this looks nothing like the pictures of Airedales Billy showed me. This puppy was completely black, and the Airedales Billy showed her were half tan and black.

"Are you sure you're giving me the right puppy?" she asked. "Were there other dogs on this flight?"

"Yes ma'am," the man answered, looking at his papers. "The other canine passengers are a German Shepherd named Ace, and a yellow Lab named Duke, both fully grown. Only one puppy on this flight from Amarillo named Henry to be delivered to a Mary Martinez, and that's you according to your papers and ID. This is your puppy," he said.

"Okay," she answered reassured, and picked up the crate with Henry stirring inside, and put it in the back of her SUV.

They only lived ten minutes from the airport, and when she carried the crate into her house, placed it on the living room floor, and opened the metal door she saw Henry wasn't moving, just lying limp in the crate.

"Oh my God," she thought, "he's dead!" and took out her cell phone and immediately called the breeder in Texas.

"Sherry, I think Henry's dead, he's not moving or breathing, just lying limp in his crate," she said frantically over the phone.

"No, he's fine," replied Sherry calmly. "He's a puppy, and they go into these deep sleeps. Airedales are hearty dogs, just take him out of his crate, shake him a bit, and when he comes to, give him some water. Call me if he doesn't wake up, but I'm sure he's fine."

Feeling reassured, she reached in and carefully lifted the limp Henry out of his crate. She could tell he was warm and breathing which made her feel better. She shook him a bit, and just like magic he came to life. He sat up and stared at this strange lady with sleepy light brown puppy eyes and gave a big yawn. She felt a jolt in her heart as their eyes connected and Henry started wagging his stubby little tail. She noticed Henry wasn't all black, he had a white patch on his chest and her heart filled with love for this tiny puppy with huge paws and tenderly said his name, "Henry."

Henry got up on all fours, shook his body, and gave himself a big long stretch after being cooped up in his carrier crate for so long, and immediately did a pee and a poo in the middle of her living room floor. Shocked out of her reverie, Billy's mom raced to get the training pads she had bought to clean up these messes, and quickly cleaned them up.

"Henry," she said. "Welcome to your new home." As Henry ran around the room to inspect his new home.

CHAPTER 3

During school lunch hour, Billy's phone beeped. He flipped it open and carefully read his mother's short text three times, before believing the words on the screen.

Henry's arrived safe and sound. He's home and dying to meet you, Mom.

The big smile on his face couldn't hide his excitement.

"What's up?" asked his friend Jamaal.

"Henry's here," he replied excitedly, scooping the rest of his frank and beans in his mouth.

"Cool!" said his friend.

The last class of the day was science, his favorite subject. Learning about plants and animals fascinated him, especially animals, as his dream was to become a veterinarian, but today the minutes dragged by like hours. He just couldn't concentrate on the lesson knowing that Henry was home. When he looked at his watch and saw only two minutes had passed since he last looked; he let out a big sigh and placed his forehead on his desk. After another excruciating thirty minutes, the bell finally rang; and he shot out of school like a rocket, hopping on his bike, and pedaling furiously home, running across streets and dodging honking cars. When he finally got home, he hopped off his bike, letting it crash on the hedge, and opened the front door. He saw Henry and his mom playing on the living room floor covered with training pads. Both stopped their play, Henry looking at him and wagging his stumpy tail, his mom with a big smile yelled, "Happy Birthday!"

Billy got down on both knees. Henry ran and jumped all over him, squealing and showering his face with licks. Billy couldn't believe what was happening; what he had waited so long for was now reality as Henry smothered every bit of his face with puppy kisses. Billy thought Henry was the most beautiful creature he had ever seen and kept saying, "Henry, Henry." As the tears rolled down his cheeks, Henry lapping them up.

"See," his mom said, "he already loves you."

"Gee, Mom," replied Billy, this is the best birthday present I've ever had in my whole life; and I promise I won't let you down. I'll do all the hard work of cleaning, feeding, training; I promise, I promise, I'll take total care of him." As Henry wriggled in his lap, Billy giving him a hug.

"Well, you can start by helping me, put his sleeping crate together." Looking at Billy and Henry, and believing his every word, at the joy on his face, knowing how hard he had worked for this day to come.

It took them more time than they thought to assemble his crate. The instructions, like Ikea furniture instructions, weren't very helpful, but through trial and error, they persisted, all the while Henry was zooming here and there, and everywhere, grabbing anything he could in his little mouth and tearing it to pieces. Cardboard, bubble wrap, Styrofoam were all fair game, but when Henry grabbed the instructions from his mom's hand, they both chased him around the messy living room, much to Henry's delight. With his crate finally assembled, Billy took Henry out to their small backyard and played with him, with one of the tug of war toys, Henry seemed to like best, growling and pulling at it like he was a ferocious dog. Billy let him win half the time, which made Henry even more engaged in the game, bringing the toy back to Billy every time he won, making Billy laugh with delight at his tough little puppy.

Soon it was supper time, and they went into the kitchen. Billy carefully measured two scoops of kibble for a ten pound puppy, and placed it into Henry's feeding bowl, filling the other bowl with fresh water. To his amazement, Henry gobbled up his kibble in seconds flat and looked at Billy for more.

"Mom, I think Henry wants more food."

"No," she said sternly. "Keep to the portions on the label so he doesn't get an upset stomach. That's what the breeder said, and don't give him any of your dinner from under the table."

His mom served him dinner, and Billy did as he was told, which was tough with Henry looking at him expectedly with his light brown puppy eyes as he ate. After dinner, they played a bit more in the backyard, chasing a ball and more tug of war. Like clockwork, after about twenty minutes, Henry did a pee and a poo which Billy diligently picked up with a poo bag and tossed it into their garbage can. Soon it was time for bed.

"Mom, can Henry sleep with me tonight?" he asked, knowing full well what the answer would be, but since it was his birthday, he thought he should give it a try.

His mother knew she had to be firm and set the rules, but she also didn't want to spoil this special day her son worked so hard for. Choosing her words carefully, she said,

"Billy, we went over this many times. Maybe when Henry gets a little older, but for now he has to get house trained and crate trained. I don't want the house covered in pee pads for months on end, and someone has to take him out to potty every two to three hours until he's about three and a half to four months and can control his bladder. Who do you think is gonna do that?"

"I will," he replied eagerly.

"Well, we'll see," she said frowning. Henry had fallen asleep under the kitchen table while Billy and his mom were talking.

"Now pick Henry up and put him in his crate next to my bed, and put that fluffy bear toy next to him so it mimics his litter mates and helps him sleep."

"Okay, mom," said Billy, gently picking Henry up, surprised to feel how limp and deep asleep he was, and carefully put him in his crate with the fluffy bear toy next to him. Billy stared lovingly at his sleeping puppy till his mother said, "C'mon Billy, off to bed. Just one more day of school and you've got Henry all to yourself for the whole weekend."

After looking at Henry one last time, Billy went to his room, hopped into bed, and fell fast asleep. His mother waking up every two hours to her cell phone alarm to take Henry out to potty. She was surprised to find that every time she placed him down on the grass in their backyard and said the word "potty." Henry would look at her, walk around, and pee or poo in the grass. Smart boy, she thought, as she'd pick him up and carry him back to his crate with no fuss or crying. She'd then look in on Billy, to find him fast asleep in bed. *Boys and puppies,* she thought, remembering her first puppy Lola, a short haired pointer she got when she was twelve. How I loved her with all my heart, my first love, and how her death tore her apart, knowing Billy would suffer the same fate when the time came. She'd read that Airedales can live up to thirteen years with exercise and a good diet. *That would take Billy to twenty-three or twenty-four,* she thought. *He'd be finished with college, be in vet school, might even be married with a family of his own.* This thought took her back to an old song her grandmother used to sing and started humming, "Que sera, sera, whatever will be will be, the future's not ours to see, que sera, sera." And set her alarm for two hours and fell asleep.

CHAPTER 4

This routine went on for the next two weeks. Henry never cried at night, liked sleeping in his crate, even in the daytime, and didn't seem to miss his mother and his litter mates, accepting Billy and his mother as his new and forever family. His mother had taken two weeks off from work to get Henry acclimated to his new home and family, and was surprised to find out how much she enjoyed spending time with him. Except for his razor sharp puppy teeth which tore holes in all her leggings and mangled his poor fluffy bear toy, she loved having Henry around while Billy was at school. Billy too kept his promise. Every morning, after feeding Henry, and cleaning his bowls, and filling them with fresh water, he'd take him for a walk around the block and pick up his poos. The same when he got home from school. Henry was toilet trained in only three days, and never did a poo in the house. The two weeks his mother took off from work really paid off with Henry's potty training and daily routines. Of course, there was plenty of puppy play time. Billy and his mother loved playing a game of making Henry know his name and come they found on YouTube. One would hide behind a tree in the backyard while Henry was in the house and yell, "Henry come!" Henry would dash out of the house to find the voice and get rewarded with a treat, while the other one would hide someplace else and yell, "Henry come!" And Henry would zoom to the sound of this voice to find it and get a treat. It only took Henry a few days to master this game and find all their hiding spots and get his treats. Henry also loved chasing balls, but wouldn't bring them back no matter how hard they tried even with treats. He preferred to chew the balls to pieces once he got them. His favorite game though was tug of war, which he could play for hours until Billy's arms got sore.

It was time for Henry's first vet visit to get his shots. While sitting in the waiting room, an elderly lady with a maltese in her lap asked Billy, "What breed is your puppy young boy; he's very cute."

"He's an Airedale terrier," replied Billy.

"He's going to be big judging by the size of those paws," she said. Her maltese not interested in Henry at all while Billy held Henry in his lap.

"Male Airedales are in the sixty-five to seventy-five pound range fully grown according to the books," said Billy.

"What's his name?" she asked.

"Henry."

"Henry?" she exclaimed inquisitively, and hearing his name looked her straight in the face.

"Why Henry, you smart little puppy, you already know your name," she gushed, making Billy feel proud of his pup.

The rest of the visit was routine. Henry was happy and wagging his tail at the vet, even when she stuck the thermometer up his rear and gave him his shots. No crying. The only surprise was when she asked, "Would you mind if my staff came in to see Henry? They've never seen an Airedale puppy before."

"Sure," said Billy and his mom in unison.

Three young staff members came into the examining

room, exclaiming how cute Henry was. Henry soaking up all the attention of the humans petting and making a fuss over him.

"See," said the vet, "Airedale puppies are all black until they're about four to five months old before their legs and face start turning tan."

"Look at the size of those paws," said one assistant.

"Yes, he's gonna be a big boy. Okay, let's all get back to work, and remember," she said to Billy and his mom, "Henry's not to meet other dogs or go near their poos until he gets his final parvo shots in three weeks. Parvo is serious and can kill puppies. Only after his final shots can you take him to the dog park to meet other dogs."

"Okay doc," replied Billy. His mom reassuring the vet they'll both keep a close eye on Henry until he gets his final shots.

It was an unusually hot day, and when they walked Henry out to the car and on the pavement, he started crying, which in itself was unusual because Henry never cried. Realizing what was wrong, Billy's mom quickly scooped Henry up in her arms, even though he was now twenty pounds, and asked Billy to feel the pavement.

"It's really hot," he said.

"Poor Henry almost had his soft puppy pads burned," she said, cuddling him in her arms. "Remember this Billy, hot pavements can burn their paws."

"I will," he said, petting and kissing Henry in his mother's arms. They took Henry home none the less for wear from his first visit to the vet.

CHAPTER 5

There were only four more weeks of school till summer vacation, then I'll have Henry every day all to myself thought Billy. Henry and Billy bonded quickly and Henry sagaciously learned what time Billy would get home from school and waited patiently for him every day at the front door. What Henry didn't know was that his dog mother's name was Ladybug, and had given birth to him and his seven siblings by caesarian in a vet clinic in Dalhart Texas. His father was Grand Champion Duke, and he was AKC registered as Henry the XVI, a purebred Airedale from excellent breeding stock. Of course, none of this mattered to Henry, the only thing that mattered to him was his boy named Billy, their play times, and how happy he was when Henry did something that made Billy happy.

On weekends, Billy decided to start training Henry, his basic commands of come, sit, down, stay, no and heel which he learned from watching Brandon McMillan on Lucky Dog, his favorite TV show. *Come* was no problem as Henry always wanted to be with Billy, and from the hide and seek game they played with his mom. *Sit* was easy too, and just like Brandon, Billy would hold a treat to Henry's nose, then raise it till Henry sat and reward him with the treat while saying, "Good boy! good boy!" With enthusiasm to let Henry know he was doing what Billy wanted him to do. *Down* was also easy, as Henry just let his nose follow the treat to the ground; *stay* took a bit more time, as did no and heel, but Henry learned them all in two days with a lot of positive reinforcement. Unknown to Billy, his mother had enrolled Henry in a puppy training class at their local Petsmart. When they took him to his first lesson, the trainer told them Henry knew all his basic commands and gave him a certificate of completion. His mother took a photo of Billy holding Henry's certificate with Henry sitting by his side. She was so proud of them she got it framed and hung it on their living room wall.

After Henry got his second parvo shot, Billy and his mom took him to their local dog park to get him socialized with other dogs. Both Billy and his mom were a little nervous when they arrived, and although Henry was only four months old and a pretty good size; the park was filled with really big dogs. Billy hesitantly opened the latch to the gate to let Henry in, when suddenly six or seven dogs came rushing to the gate barking wildly to meet Henry, who was wagging his tail and barking happily to meet his new friends. Billy's mom quickly took control of the situation and walked through the gate with her arms down and palms open, blocking the dogs inside from running out, and that's when Henry saw his chance and bolted in. With his long legs, Henry raced to the far end of the park, a good fifty yards; the other dogs running and barking happily at the chase, though none could catch him. Henry then turned around and doubled back in the opposite direction and back again in pure joy with the rest of the pack chasing him with wild abandon. After doing this a few times he stopped, and all the dogs surrounded and gave him a good sniff, while Henry did the same. Then suddenly one of the other dogs bolted and the chase was on again, with Henry joining his new friends.

"Well, I guess he's socialized," said his mom in amazement of Henry.

"Yeah, guess so, mom," replied Billy in awe of how fast and athletic Henry was.

After the second chase ended, Henry started play fighting with a young boxer his size; the other dogs losing interest and going about their own business. A young woman in her twenties came up to Billy's mom and asked, "What breed of dog Henry was."

"You tell her, Billy," said his mom.

"He's an Airedale Terrier," said Billy.

"An Airedale," she replied. "I've never seen one before. He's really beautiful."

"Thanks," said Billy and his mom.

"What's his name?"

"Henry," answered Billy.

"That boxer he's playing with is Tucker; he's my dog. Tucker's four and a half months old and it looks like they're gonna be good friends."

"Henry's a little over four months," said Billy. And all three watched Henry and Tucker play fighting for half an hour, entertaining them with all their puppy antics. They stood on their hind legs and box each other, then laid down on the grass and fight like cats on their backs, only to get up and grab each other by the neck or leg to pull each other to the ground. His mother started talking with the other dog parents at the park, and when it was time to go, Tucker wouldn't let Henry leave, jumping on his back, letting one leg hang over him like a human putting an arm around a best friend. Of course Henry obliged, wanting nothing more than more play time with his new best friend.

"Oh, let him play a bit more," said his mom. "He's having so much fun, dinner can wait an extra half hour," and Billy let Henry off his leash to resume playing with Tucker. This became Henry's evening routine, dinner, then a walk to the dog park to play with Tucker, his new best doggy friend.

Chapter 6

Like all childhood summers, this one passed quickly. June, July and August were filled with long morning walks and evening trips to the dog park. One morning, while Billy and Henry were walking through an empty field which stretched into open desert that his mom told him not to go because of rattlesnakes and coyotes. Henry spotted a jackrabbit and the chase was on. Billy stood in amazement as Henry let out a high pitched yell and chased the jackrabbit up a steep canyon wall disappearing over the rim. Billy got worried with not being able to see Henry and started running up the canyon wall when he heard a single bark, as if saying he got away, then saw Henry trotting over the rim and returning to him.

"Good boy," gushed Billy, "you showed that jackrabbit who's the boss and came back. Good boy!"

This was a secret he and Henry would keep to themselves until the cool weather arrived, and the rattlesnakes went into hibernation. Coyotes were a different problem, as all the recent housing development brought them close to the city and parks in search of food. His mother had showed him a YouTube video about the dangers of coyotes; and why she didn't want them walking in the desert. In it a small terrier is seen, barking at a doggy door in someone's house, when suddenly in the blink of an eye a coyote rushed in, grabbed the small dog in its mouth and disappeared. Billy knew Henry was too big for a coyote to grab for a quick meal, but still, the video of the poor little terrier disturbed him.

"Promise me, you won't go walking in the desert with Henry. You can see how dangerous coyotes are," she warned.

"Promise," replied Billy. Although he hated lying to his mom, and this troubled him deeply as they were so close. He saw how Henry came to life in the rabbit chases. How his natural hunting instincts fulfilled him in the chase and brought him joy. Billy was glad he couldn't catch them, as killing animals and hunting animals for fun turned his stomach. He and his mother were staunch animal lovers, and Billy even tried to be a vegetarian a few times because he felt sorry for the animals like cows, pigs, and sheep that were farmed for humans to eat. Nothing disturbed him more on road trips with his mom than when they'd pass a cattle truck stuffed with cows standing shoulder to shoulder with no room to move on the way to the slaughterhouse. His longest vegetarianism lasted almost six months, until he joined his friends one afternoon to an in In-N-Out Burger, and he couldn't resist the temptation. Although not a vegetarian, he liked that he and his mom practiced no meat Mondays and fish Fridays limiting their consumption of meat. Vegetarian curries, pizzas, and fish and chips ruled the no meat days.

By the end of summer, Henry grew big and strong from all the walks, rabbit chases, and playfighting with Tucker in the evenings. Unlike most dogs who walk with their noses to the ground to pick up smells, Henry stood upright and erect, and with his long legs, this gave him a noble and majestic bearing. Never a week went by when someone would complement Billy on what a beautiful dog he had. Often asking what breed was Henry. Once, a bus stopped, and the driver opened his doors and yelled, "Hey kid, what kind of a dog is that?"

"He's an Airedale Terrier," Billy yelled back at this bus stopped in the middle of the street.

"I've seen you two walking around the neighborhood together, and he looks so cool. I've gotta get me one," yelled the bus driver, as he closed his doors and drove off, making Billy feel proud of his best friend.

Henry also had a longer snout than most Airedales, the reason his mother would sometimes call him "wolfy" one of their many pet names for him. On her days off and weekends, she sometimes joined them on their walks, often taking them to dog friendly cafes for breakfast where waitstaff would always faun all over Henry, asking if they could give him strips of bacon and pet him. Henry was a star; and Billy knew he was special; and his mom loved how Henry made them a family.

It was almost ten years since her husband and Billy's father had died in Afghanistan. After 9/11 he was caught up in the patriotic war fervor that ran across America like a wild fire. He enlisted in the army at twenty-two and was dead at twenty-four, killed by an I.U.D. while patrolling the streets of Kabul, leaving her a widow at twenty-three, and Billy fatherless at just under two. She remembered them being the happiest days of her life when Billy was born and before he joined the army. She had begged him not to join and stay at home with their perfect little family, but being the child of Filipino immigrants, he wanted to fight the war on terror to show how much he loved America. He paid with his life. Her grief at times was almost too much to bear. The physical pain of seeing him return in a flag draped coffin causing her knees to buckle and made her collapse at the sight. She found his funeral surreal, like an out of body experience not really happening to her; but with a toddler on her hands and starting a new job fresh out of nursing school, her busy life helped her cope with his loss. '*You never get over it*,' she had read in a book on grief by Elisabeth Kubler-Ross; but you do get through it, and learn to live with the loss, which she did. This feeling of family that Henry had given them made her love him as much as Billy. While Billy was at school, she would often take Henry on errands at the dog friendly stores like Lowe's or Home Depot where the staff and customers always complimented what a good dog he was. She trained Henry to sit in the back seat of her SUV like a person; and Henry enjoyed sitting and looking out the window at the world passing by, never barking or sticking his head out like other dogs.

"Like three peas in a pod," she'd always say smiling when they were together. Life was good again.

CHAPTER 7

By the time September rolled in, Henry grew big and strong, and at six months was eighty percent of his adult size. Along with the cooler weather, the new school year, this year would be different. Billy would be starting seventh grade in Jr. High School. His new school was miles away from his house. He'd have to take the bus, but his mom said she'd drive him and pick him up in the afternoons for the first two weeks of school to get his routine started on the right foot. He dreaded having to leave Henry alone while he was at school, as they had bonded so closely over the summer, spending every moment of the day together. At night, Henry was now allowed to sleep with Billy in his bedroom, bonding them even closer. His mother reassured him; Henry would be okay, as he was older now, and depending on her shifts at the hospital, would be home with him a lot of the time. Still, as the first day of school approached, Billy's anxiety of leaving Henry and going to a new school grew.

The first day of Jr. High School arrived, and Billy got dressed in the new jeans and shirt his mother bought. He wasn't too crazy about his mom picking his clothes for him, but they compromised on him not getting a haircut. He wanted to keep it long, and she acquiesced as long as he kept it clean and neat. She actually liked the way his long black hair looked. Billy had a MopTop which reminded her of her mother's favorite group the Beatles. Billy sort of looking like an adolescent Filipino Paul McCartney. She knew he'd be popular with the girls with his big brown almond shaped eyes and small even features, looking more Asian like his dad than her.

"Well," she said. "Ready?"

"Yeah, I guess so," replied Billy mournfully.

Henry sensed something was up this morning, and his intelligent light brown eyes kept darting from one to the other, seeming to follow their conversation.

"Oh, he can come for the ride," she said.

"Really?" said Billy, all smiles now. "C'mon, boy." And they all piled into his mom's SUV.

They drove to his new school in silence. Henry sitting in the back, looking out the window, taking in the scenery like a human. When they got to the school, which was a big three-story building. Billy grabbed his backpack, kissed his mom goodbye, and reached back giving Henry a pat on the head. He walked to the entrance; his mom's and Henry's eyes following him until he disappeared into the throng of students at the front door. Henry gave a whimper when he could no longer see Billy. His mom looked back and said, "It'll be okay, boy. He'll be home later." And Henry looked her in the eyes, knowing this was okay, and settled down.

Billy followed the students; the teachers directing them into the auditorium, when he saw his friend Jamaal and a girl named Sally from his old school and sat in an empty chair next to them. The principal, a youngish friendly looking woman was on the stage, welcoming them to their new school. She briefly told them the rules they were to follow and the layout of the school, before handing out their home-room cards with class schedules and dismissing assembly.

Billy was relieved to find he was in the same homeroom as Jamaal and Sally. The three of them found their homeroom on the second floor and sat in desks next to each other with seventeen other strangers from different schools in the room. Their homeroom teacher briefly went over what the principal told them in assembly, but with more detail and took attendance. Billy liked their homeroom teacher as she came across warm and friendly, and also turned out to be his English teacher. The buzzer rang, and they all filed out to their first classes of the day. Billy's had Math class in room 214, which he found easily. His new school was three stories, with most classrooms on the second and third floors, with the gym, cafeteria, and offices on the first floor.

Although, he was a good student, his only thought was to get home to Henry. This is so different from grade school he thought, as now he had to get to different classes with different teachers, whereas before, he stayed in the same classroom with the same teacher for the whole semester. Plus, he only had two minutes when the buzzer rang to get from classroom to classroom.

When his mom picked him up that afternoon, he ran to the car; he saw Henry sitting in the back seat. His mom opened the door to let Henry out as he was getting too excited and ran to meet Billy, jumping all over him, giving out excited yelps and smothering his face with licks.

"Henry, Henry," Billy cried out, hugging his bundle of love that was jumping all over him. "Oh how I missed you, boy. Let's go home and go for a walk." Life was perfect.

CHAPTER 8

It wasn't until a few weeks later the trouble began. A big white kid in gym class started picking on him, calling him racist names like chink, spic, gook, browny. It was Billy's first encounter with a bully and racism. This troubled him deeply. He couldn't understand why someone he didn't even know hated him for the way he looked and the color of his skin. It began innocently enough in English class when their teacher asked them to write and recite a short essay about themselves. Like most kids, Billy hated public speaking. He wrote a few paragraphs, and when the dreaded day arrived, he went up nervously to the front of the class and waited until his teacher gave him the nod to speak. He took a deep breath and said, "My name is Billy Martinez. I live with my mom who's a nurse, and my best friend Henry who's an Airedale Terrier. I never knew my dad. He was in the army and killed in Afghanistan when I was two. Except from photos and what my mom told me about him, I know he was from New York, Astoria Queens, was a NY Yankees fan, and I am too. I don't have any hobbies and spend most of my spare time helping my mom and going for long walks with Henry."

Billy was interrupted by someone in the rear of the class making kissing noises and saying, "Mama," in a high squeaky doll's voice. This made some of the kids laugh.

"Shush, whoever's making those noises," said their

teacher. "You show everyone in this class respect or I'm gonna flunk whoever it is that's behaving like an idiot. Now go on, Billy."

Flustered, Billy continued, "I help my mom with grocery shopping, laundry, keeping my room clean and taking care of Henry, feeding, brushing, and cleaning him. For this, she treats me to an In-N-Out Burger once a week. Henry gets one too, but with no cheese or fries. When I grow up, I want to be a veterinarian because I love animals. I know I should be a vegetarian because I don't like the idea of animals suffering in pens and being killed just so we can eat them. I read that they're sentient beings, which means they have feelings. That's why I try to eat meat only two or three times a week, which isn't that hard because pizza is my favorite food."

"What a wimp," came a muted voice from the rear of the room.

"Whoever said that, this is your last warning. If I find out who you are, I'll not only flunk you, but send you down to the office where your parents can pick you up after detention." This threat made the class so quiet you could hear a pin drop.

"That's very admirable of you, Billy," said their teacher after a few moments. "I've also tried to become a vegetarian for the same reasons and got as far as three months when the smell of bacon while visiting my parents got the better of me."

This made the class laugh, releasing the tension in the room. "Any more, Billy?" she asked.

"No ma'am, that's it."

"Okay, let's give Billy a hand." And the class applauded as Billy returned to his seat.

When Billy sat down, his friend Jamaal whispered to

him, "It's that big kid Cody in the back making the kissing noises. You better watch out man, cause that kid's trouble. His dad owns a garage and keeps pit bulls for protection."

"Thanks man," whispered Billy, wondering why some kid he didn't know was making fun of him.

The next day in gym class, they were playing three-on-three basketball. Cody was on the team, playing against Billy. Billy got a pass and drove to the basket for an easy lay up, when Cody grabbed him from behind and threw him violently to the floor. Sprawled on the ground and stunned, Cody stood over him and shouted, "Get up, Gook, you brown faced chink, get up."

Billy looked for Mr. Johnson their gym teacher, but he was at the other end of the gym supervising other kids.

"C'mon, Browny, you fucking wimp," sneered Cody. Billy was both shocked and frightened, not knowing what to do. None of the other boys came to his defense, just standing around, not wanting to get involved. At nearly six feet tall and 175 pounds they were all frightened of him. Deciding not to say anything and afraid to look Cody in the eyes, Billy slowly got up, when he heard Mr. Johnson say, "C'mon you boys, why are you all standing around? Let's go, we're here to play."

They finished their game. Cody's team won. Billy's team, frightened of the bully content to shoot jump shots with no driving to the basket or fighting for rebounds. As they walked to the shower room, Cody walked by Billy and sneered in his ear, "You're my bitch, now you wimp."

Frightened and confused by this turn of events, Billy just wanted to get home and be with Henry. He was too embarrassed and ashamed to tell anyone he was being bullied at school.

CHAPTER 9

"Mom," he asked her the next morning, "I think I'd like to learn karate."

"That's a great idea," she said before sipping her cup of coffee. "Y'know your dad was a third degree blackbelt in Tae Kwon Do, and he was pretty good at it. He even taught it at Prudential Securities down on Wall Street in New York. It'll be good for you, get your body strong, mind focused, teach you discipline and respect. I've got the weekend off, so we can check out a few schools tomorrow."

"Cool," replied Billy, not telling her the real reason he wanted to learn karate.

On Saturday morning, she had a list of some schools nearby. They all hopped into her car to check them out with Henry. The first few were for kids only. Billy didn't like them. He thought they were too soft and the instructors pandered to the children and their parents. The last school on her list was for adults, but kids were allowed if they were twelve and over. It was taught by an old Korean master Mr. Sun, and Billy liked the idea if being taught by an Asian master. He and his mom sat in chairs in the front of the Dojang with Henry sitting at their feet. Billy was in awe as Mr. Sun put the lines of blackbelts and lower belts through a variety of kicks, punches and blocks with speed and strength during their basics. When they all yelled "utz" in unison after a kick or punch, Billy felt inspired. Henry barked.

"This is the class I want to join," he told his mom, and she enrolled him in classes twice a week.

Mr. Sun didn't suffer fools or have favorites. Having taught the cadets at West Point for a few years before opening his own school he was strictly business. "Work hard, strong kick, strong punch, stay focus, too slow," he'd admonish his students in broken English while putting them through their motions. "Too slow, weak," he'd tell students that didn't meet his expectations when kicking or punching the bags. After Billy learned his basics and Kuk Mu forms in three weeks, he got his yellow belt and was now allowed to free style spar. Mr. Sun's method for sparring was to have all the higher ranking blackbelts in descending order in one line, and all the lower ranking belts from yellow, green, purple and brown facing them in another line. This way the novices learned from the best. Billy was nervous facing a fourth degree blackbelt who was one of the best. Mr. Sun clapped his hands to begin, but before Billy had time to get into a fighting stance, got a spinning side kick a quarter inch from his face at full force, quickly followed by a roundhouse kick to the side of his head. *"Whoa,"* Billy thought, *"this guy's dangerous."* But before he could get another thought in his head Mr. Sun yelled, "Fight, fight, fight. "Which Billy tried to do, only to get a left sidekick, a fraction from his gut, instinctively forcing him back, only to have the blackbelt spin on the floor with his leg extended sweeping Billy on his back. On his back, Billy was stunned and didn't know what to do, but before another thought could enter his startled mind, Mr. Sun started yelling, "Up, up, fight, fight." Billy got up and tried to throw a left sidekick, but it was too slow, easily blocked by the blackbelt who countered with a right sidekick to his mouth, the dust from the floor settling in his lips making him want to spit. Mr. Sun clapped his hands which was the signal to stop, get in line, and bow to your partner. Billy moved down to the next blackbelt. This one didn't have the fancy spinning kicks but was huge and strong. Billy felt like a fly trying to fight a gorilla. This humiliation and character building continued for the next half hour until it was time for warm downs and the end of the class. There were only two other kids in the class, a fifteen-year-old purple belt, and a seventeen-year-old brown belt.

The purple belt came up to him in the dressing room and said, "Don't worry first free style is always the hardest, but it gets you to learn how to fight really fast. We all began the same way, you'll be fine." No one else spoke a word to him. Billy appreciated his kind words, got dressed, determined to be good.

Knowing the level of competency, he'd have to learn to be a good fighter. Billy began jogging instead of walking with Henry every day, which Henry didn't seem to mind, especially when Billy would run full speed at the end of their jogs. He started doing pushups. Four reps of ten to begin with, increasing to four reps of twenty, to four reps of fifty by the end of the month. The same with his crunches. Like all young people who work out he built muscle fast. His flat belly turning into a washboard. His chest and arms like steel. What Billy lacked in size, he was only 5' 5" and 105 pounds; he made up with in speed and flexibility. He stretched every day and soon could do full splits. By the time he got his purple belt, he was holding his own in sparring, and he was limber enough to throw a sidekick to the face of a six footer. Mr. Sun never complimented him, but the other blackbelts started talking to him and teaching him how to do reverse spin and sidekicks, as well as using his hip to add acceleration and force to his roundhouse kicks. Perhaps the most important lesson of all was from Mr. Sun when he'd talk to the class before dismissing them.

"Many bad boys and bullies out there. You never fight unless have to." Mr. Sun would point to his biceps, which were still big for his age and say, "Bad boy here strong." Then point to his other bicep, "Here strong." Then point to his heart and head and say, "But here weak, here weak." Then point to the class, "But you strong everywhere because work hard, strong kick, strong punch, strong mind, strong heart, focus, show respect, all good boys and girls." Which made men and women in their forties and older smile and laugh, as he was like a surrogate father to them all, and they got a kick out of being called boys and girls.

At school, Billy avoided Cody like the plague. If he saw him walking down the hall, he'd turn the other way. In gym stayed close to Mr. Johnson. In the cafeteria, wait until he saw Cody and his friends sit down, then get his lunch and sit as far away as possible. The few times he couldn't avoid him Cody would walk up to him and sneer at his face calling him bitch, chink, gook, browny, his friends laughing as Billy walked away in silence, refusing to respond to Cody's racial slurs. He was no longer physically afraid of Cody, but was a firm believer of Mr. Sun's philosophy of *you don't fight unless you have to*. Walk away unless there's no other option. Mr. Sun would tell them if they had to fight, "bad boy no gentleman, he want hurt you, you no fight like gentleman, kick and punch fast, hard. Good Tae Kwon Do one or two combinations, more than bad Tae Kwon Do. No gentleman fight in street. Kick here, punch here, never punch in head or break hand, axe hand in neck, side kick in ribs good, no muscle in neck and ribs. Then walk away."

CHAPTER 10

Billy's routine was set for the rest of the semester. Long morning jogs and runs with Henry every morning in the canyons, school from nine to three, another shorter run and jog after school, and Tae Kwon Do classes Wednesdays and Saturdays.

One day on one of their morning jogs, Henry spotted a jackrabbit and went running after it while emitting a high pitched yelp. Billy watched him disappear over a canyon wall, then heard him give one loud bark, as if to say damn it, he got away. He then watched Henry trot over the canyon wall and return. "Good boy," said Billy. "You really are a hunting dog." They continued their jog and every now and then, if Henry saw a jackrabbit, he'd give it a chase with his high pitched yelp. Billy happy to stand and watch Henry have his fun, thankful he never caught and killed one.

Every now and then, after their evening runs, Billy would take Henry to the dog park to play with Tucker. They still loved play fighting with each other, but not as much as when they were younger, both growing out of that young puppy stage.

One afternoon, after a longer than usual run, Billy decided to take him to the dog park to play with Tucker. There weren't any rabbits to chase that afternoon and Billy thought Henry would like to blow off some steam and have a play. When they got to the park it was empty. Strange, thought Billy, to see the park with no dogs or people. It was only a half hour later than the usual time they got there. He let Henry through the gate, and that's when Billy realized his mistake. He saw Cody walking down the path with a pit bull that had its' ears cut short like a fighting dog.

"Hey mama's boy," shouted Cody. "Let's see what you and your bitch dog can do now chink that no one's around."

They were trapped.

CHAPTER 11

Henry sensed something was wrong. Instead of running to the gate to greet the new dog coming in, he stayed by Billy's side. Henry gave two loud barks. Billy looked him in the eyes and said, "Stay boy." Looking into Henry's intelligent eyes, Billy knew Henry understood this wasn't going to be play. It was at this point Cody unlatched the second gate, entered the dog park, and yelled, "Sic 'em boy." His pit bull shooting like a rocket towards them.

"Run Henry, run," yelled Billy with urgency, and like Henry did those many months ago when he first came to the park with Billy and his mom, bolted to the far end of the park, the pit bull in hot pursuit. When Henry got to the far end of the park, he easily eluded the pit bull and ran to the opposite end at full speed. The pit bull no match for Henry's long legs and graceful strides. Fifty yards later, Henry did the same thing and doubled back, Billy yelling, "Go boy go." Cody yelling, "Get him, sic 'im."

This chase went on for seven more laps, then Henry ran to one corner of the park which had benches and tables and stopped. The pit bull came up panting heavily and cornered him. Billy was worried. Cody, seeing Henry cornered, and sensing blood screamed at his dog, "Get him, kill him."

Billy started to run towards them to save Henry, when he saw Henry do something he thought only happened in movies. Cornered, the pit bull charged at Henry, but Henry gracefully with his long legs jumped four feet over the pit bull like a gymnast, the pit bull also jumped to bite him in the air, but when he clamped his jaws, got nothing but air, and the chase was on again.

They ran five more laps around the park when the pit bull just stopped, giving up, and lay on the grass with all four legs splayed and panting profusely. Henry also stopped, stood near the pit bull hardly panting at all, seemingly with a smile on his face.

"Good for nothing bitch dog," cursed Cody, walking over and kicking his dog in the rear. The pit bull yelped in pain and crawled under a table to get away from Cody.

"Your dog may get away with not fighting, but not you chink. Now you're mine," sneered Cody angrily, walking towards Billy. Henry growled at the approaching Cody, but Billy said, "Stay boy, stay," and Henry did as he was told.

"I don't want any trouble, man," said Billy, as Cody got closer.

"It's too late for that, Browny," replied Cody, now within fighting distance.

Mr. Sun's voice came into Billy's head, "If you have no option and have to fight, hit hard. Hit fast. Use combinations, fight over, walk away."

Cody threw a right punch at Billy's face, which he easily evaded by stepping back and taking one step to the side, allowing him to fire a lightning quick roundhouse kick into Cody's gut, surprised to see how easily this made this boy twice his size double over in pain, clutching his stomach.

"No more," said Billy. "I don't wanna fight any more." But Cody straightened up, rushing him like a football player, grabbing him with both arms on top like a tackle. Using Cody's forward motion force, Billy rolled on his back and with both legs coiled in a crunch, released them like springs, sending Cody flying in the air and flipping over so that he landed on his face, eating a mouthful of dirt. Dazed but not hurt. Cody got up to continue the fight, refusing to let Billy get the better of him. Mr. sun's voice once again came into Billy's head. "Combination. Combination. Finish fight and walk away." As Cody approached, all of Mr. Sun's teachings came into his head. "No such thing gentleman fight in street. If bad boy come to hurt you, hit fast, hit hard. Good Tae Kwon Do two or three combinations." Billy knew what to do as Cody got closer and sneered, "You piece of shit, Gook." With his left leg, Billy gave him a full force side kick in the gut, as Cody crumbled forward holding his stomach, with his right leg gave Cody a front kick to his face, which exploded like a watermelon, blood flying everywhere. The force of the front kick landing Cody on his back out cold. Billy walked over to make sure he was breathing, and said to Henry, "C'mon boy, let's go home." Walking out, he saw Cody's pit bull licking the blood off Cody's face.

The next day in school, Cody was absent. Billy worried about someone finding out about their fight and getting into trouble. When Cody didn't turn up for the whole week, this eased his mind as the following week began the Christmas holidays, and there'd be no school for ten days. Billy didn't tell a soul about their fight.

When school resumed in January, Billy noticed some of the kids started looking at him differently. Cody was back at school, but seemed to avoid him, which was fine with

Billy. At the end of their first week back, Jamaal sat with him during lunch hour and asked, "Is it true?"

"Is what true?" replied Billy.

"C'mon, man, don't mess with me," said Jamaal annoyed. "Is it true you kicked Cody's ass and sent him to the hospital?"

Sheepishly Billy confessed, "Yeah, I beat him up; but I had no choice; he cornered me; and Henry in the dog park with his pit bull; and I didn't want to fight; I didn't know…"

Jamaal cutting him off said, "I knew it, I knew it, my man Billy, the most dangerous kid in Jr High. No wonder everyone's giving you respect, you're one bad dude, a regular Jet Li."

"It's not like that, man," said Billy with humility. "I was forced to fight and had to defend myself."

"Whatever, dude, but whatever you did, you kicked the bully right out of that asshole. He's like everyone's best friend now, Mr. nice guy," said Jamaal, beaming with pride at his friend.

The rest of the school year passed without any dramas. Billy got all A's and some B's on his report card. They celebrated Henry's first and Billy's thirteenth birthdays. Billy continued studying Tae Kwon Do with Mr. Sun, advancing to brown belt and beginning the two year preparation period for his blackbelt test. Cody became one of the friendliest and nicest kids in school. As Jamaal had said, knocking the bully out of him. But most of all, Billy and Henry got to do what they both loved doing the most. Going on long walks and jogs, chasing jackrabbits, and simply being together. As summer vacation began, Billy thought life couldn't get any better.

CHAPTER 12

Billy and Henry's second summer together proved even more enjoyable than their first. Henry was now fully grown at eighty-five pounds. Billy grew three inches taller to 5'6" and weighed one hundred and fourteen pounds. Both were full of muscle from all their walks, jogs and runs. The dog park and canyons were at the foothills of the Sierra Nevada range. They started trekking deeper on the trails, and sometimes where the trails ended and the vegetation more abundant, the air got noticeably cooler. They'd get up early before sunrise, Billy filling his backpack with an apple and container of water for himself and Henry to share where they'd stop, then head back home. At three thousand feet the scrub began to turn to small trees and farther up at five thousand feet the pine forest began.

"One day when it's cooler, we'll get up there boy," he told Henry, sitting next to him on a rock. Billy took out the apple, bit out a big chunk and gave it to Henry before taking a bite for himself. After they ate their apple, Billy took out their container of water and with the little disk that looked like a frisbee, opened it up till it became a bowl, filled it with water, and held it for Henry to lap up, before drinking some himself. It was always Henry first with Billy, as his love for his dog knew no bounds.

"Okay, boy. Let's head back home before it gets too hot," he told Henry, putting the empty water container and drinking bowl into his now light backpack. He always liked the way down, as it was faster, and he could get into a fast run to get more exercise on their excursions. When they got near the town, civilization as Billy called it, the scrub flattened out and Henry took off for a chase. Those are pretty big ears thought Billy, watching two pairs of ears hopping up and down from the top of the scrubs. His heart stopped when he realized what he thought were jackrabbits were actually coyotes with Henry in hot pursuit.

"Henry stay, stay!" he yelled at the top of his voice and started running as fast as he could after them. Although Billy was now taller and faster, he was no match for Henry and the coyotes and kept losing ground.

"Henry stay! Stay!" he kept yelling in desperation. Suddenly the two coyotes ran up a small mound and stopped. Henry finally stopping at the base of the mound. In the few seconds it took for Billy to catch up, the two coyotes started howling with their muzzles straight up in the air. Just like in the movies, thought Billy, when suddenly five more coyotes appeared out of nowhere. Joining the two at the top of the mound. Billy noticed two of the coyotes were much bigger, German Shepherd size, and now they were staring at him and Henry growling with anger in their eyes. His mind kept repeating the vision of the little terrier in his kitchen barking at the doggy door when like a flash a coyote shoots through grabbing the little terrier in its' mouth and gone.

Billy didn't know what to do. Henry kept growling and barking back, looking at Billy as if to say let me at them, with no fear of being outnumbered at all. Billy slowly attached his leash to his collar to prevent Henry from rushing up the mound to fight and certain death. While the growling standoff continued, Billy looked around them, there were no sticks, but he saw a few big rocks, and slowly bent down, picking one up, all the while with his other hand holding on to Henry who was tugging at his leash wanting to fight.

Although he'd never been in a situation like this, something in his mind told him to move slowly. Mr. Sun's voice came in his head. Always fight the leader and the others will run away. He kept his eyes fixed on the two biggest coyotes snarling at them.

"Easy boy, easy. Stay," he told Henry as calmly as he could. He slowly started backing up away from the mound. Luckily, he thought, the coyotes didn't move and stayed on the top of the mound snarling, but not charging. With every step backwards, he could hear his heart beating like a bass drum, louder than all the snarling and growling going on. Because of the rough and scrubby terrain, it felt like hours before they were able to double the distance between them and the coyotes. His mind kept telling him if they attacked, get the big ones first.

The desert sun was now up and beating down on them. Although it felt like hours to cover only twenty-five yards, he was sweating profusely. He thought they could turn their backs on the coyotes and slowly walk away. Something in his mind told him not to run, just walk, they didn't want to be chased by wild and hungry animals. Walking away, he kept turning his back to make sure the coyotes weren't chasing and when they got to fifty yards he turned around and the coyotes were gone. Disappeared into thin air. He stopped and looked at Henry and said, "Whew! That was a close one boy." And bent down, wrapping his arms around Henry. "Don't you ever go chasing coyotes again. I thought we were goners for sure," and walked home.

The rest of the summer had no such dramas. Billy kept a keen eye out for coyotes; and Henry entertained himself by chasing jackrabbits. This childhood summer flew by just as fast as the previous one. Soon the cooler weather would bring in the beginning of fall and a new school year. As the first day of school approached, Billy wondered what he'd be learning in the eighth grade. He never told his mother about their encounter with the coyotes, just like he'd never told anyone about his fight with Cody.

"This is between you and me, boy," he told Henry, patting him on the head and kissing his face. "You and me." Henry giving his face a nice big lick in return.

CHAPTER 13

It was a few weeks before the start of the new school year. Billy started noticing his mother wearing more makeup and perfume. A few nights ago, she told him she was going out with friends after work, which he assumed were with her girlfriends. He didn't mind this at all because on those nights she went out, she ordered pizza delivered for him and he could watch whatever he wanted on TV, which was usually baseball.

Two weeks after school started and he got his new classes and schedule, she told him she wanted him to meet someone. "Sure," said Billy, not thinking anything of it.

"No," she replied seriously. "I want you to meet someone special."

"Oh, okay," he replied, a bit surprised.

"I've started seeing someone. A young doctor at the hospital. I've told him all about you, Henry, me being a widow and single mom and all that, and it hasn't scared him off. It's been ten years since your dad died, and I think this thing with Steve, that's his name, is starting to get serious, and he wants to meet you and Henry."

"Sure, mom," replied Billy sheepishly. He was a little surprised at this turn of events, but happy for his mom who hardly dated and never brought men home. Henry sitting and listening attentively, looking back and forth from one face to the other as if following their conversation, sensing the mood.

"This Saturday, then," said his mom smiling. "I'll be making dinner and Steve'll be over at six. Just make sure you're home from Tae Kwon Do and taken Henry out for his walk. He's dying to meet the both of you."

"Yeah, of course, mom," replied Billy. "Just as long as he makes you happy and you deserve to be happy," he said, giving his mom a big hug.

"Thanks dear, Oh how I love you," she replied blissfully, wrapping her arms around him, her eyes misting with tears. Henry stood up on his hind legs and licking their faces, not wanting to be left out of their love session.

Saturday came and the doorbell rang. Henry rushed to the door barking loudly, warning any intruders he was on guard. His mom opened the door and Steve walked in hesitantly as Henry stood his ground, preventing him from fully entering. "It's okay Henry, he's a friend," she told him, Steve standing still and letting Henry sniff him all over.

"I didn't think he'd be this big or have such a loud bark," he said to his mom, who was smiling at him.

"I'll take that," she said, grabbing the bottle of wine from his hand while Henry continued his sniffing inspection. After a minute or so Steve passed Henry's muster and let him walk into the house.

"Hi, I'm Steve," he said to Billy smiling, extending his hand for a shake. "Your mom's told me all about you and Henry."

"Hi," replied Billy, shaking his hand while surveying his mom's boyfriend. He was a little taller than average, maybe 5'10" thought Billy, with short thick sandy colored close cropped hair and wearing nerdy glasses. But he had a friendly face, the kind patients like. He looked younger than he imagined. His mother was thirty-seven, but she looked ten years younger. Some people mistook her for his sister which always embarrassed him, but at 5'7" with long straight light brown hair with blond highlights and full of youthful energy it was easy to see why. They make a nice looking couple, he thought, looking at them standing together. He watched his mom give Steve, a kiss. He'd never seen his mom kiss another man before. He knew this was serious.

During dinner Steve asked Billy all about his dream of becoming a vet. Why he wanted to be one, his grades, the competition of getting into vet school tougher than medical school because there were fewer of them etc. He took a keen interest in Billy's answers, encouraging him to keep up with his grades, especially science as that would determine whether he'd get in or not. His mother kept silent, letting them get to know each other, but smiling proudly at Billy's answers. After dinner he took Henry out for his walk so Steve and his mom could be alone. Returning an hour later, he was surprised to see Steve had gone.

"That went well," she said beaming, as Billy and Henry walked into the kitchen. "He thinks you're a terrific young man and very mature for your age."

"Well, I like him too, mom. I'm glad he makes you happy," he replied giving his mom a hug. Henry again jumping up on both of them, not wanting to be left out of this happy moment. This made them both laugh out loud at this three-way hug.

Steve soon became a regular fixture at their house. In the beginning only once or twice a week. Later, spending nights, then whole weekends. They spent Christmas together, Billy learning Steve came from Philadelphia, that both his parents died in a car crash in his sophomore year in college, and that he had an older sister mom's age who was married with two children and living in Boston. Billy was right about Steve being younger than his mom at thirty, but they looked the same age and were very happy together. The seven-year-age difference didn't seem to matter to them. They were four now. Steve was there to celebrate Henry's second birthday and Billy's fourteenth. Billy's grades were mostly A's, and he learned his new forms for his blackbelt test. Everything was going fine when a week after his birthday his mother dropped the bombshell.

CHAPTER 14

"Steve's asked me to marry him," she said when he came home from school.

"Why that's great, mom!" he replied happy for her, but sensed something wasn't right from the expression on her face.

"It's the second part you're not going to like," she said seriously, motioning for him to sit down on the sofa. Billy put down his backpack at the same time Henry jumped on the sofa and welcomed him home.

"He's been offered a job in Hawaii, in a good hospital in Honolulu."

"That's great, mom, what's wrong with that?" he asked, perplexed by her demeanor.

"Hawaii doesn't have rabies Billy. It means Henry will have to be in quarantine for six months."

Billy's heart dropped. The words quarantine and six months hitting him like a sidekick to the gut. His mother knew this was going to be tough, but was now concerned by the look on her son's face. Tears started flowing down his cheeks and Henry started licking them up, unaware the conversation was about him.

"I know this is a big sacrifice, Billy; and six months is an awful long time, but you'll be able to visit him after the first two weeks." Trying her best to put a positive spin on this most difficult situation. Knowing how much Billy loved Henry, that Henry was more of a friend than a dog to Billy. She loved Henry too, and nothing made her happier than seeing how much they loved being together, and how Henry had made them a family again. Three peas in a pod.

Her words weren't registering in his mind. His body feeling totally numb. He put his arms around Henry who was busy licking the tears from his face. He sat there stone faced before finally saying, "Six months mom! That's like almost four years in a dog's life."

"I know, I know, but think of the wonderful life the two of you will have when he gets out. We'll be in Hawaii, Henry can become a beach dog, long walks along the shore, swimming together, you can learn to surf and take him with you. This will be a fresh start for all of us –a new beginning. Now I haven't given Steve my answer yet. I told him I'd have to run it by you first, and if you don't want to go, then we'll stay here. You know I'll never love anyone as much as I love you. Steve comes second, but I really want to go. I do love him and I think this will be a great opportunity for us all. He's told the hospital in Hawaii if he accepts the position, he wouldn't be able to start until September. That way you can finish the school year here, take your blackbelt test with Mr. Sun, and start the new school year in Hawaii. I want you to think about this carefully before I give Steve my answer. This means a lot to me, and although I really want to go, if you don't, then we stay here."

"Okay, mom," replied a stunned Billy. He got up, grabbed his trekking backpack, threw an apple and granola bar in it with their container of water, zipped it, and said, "We're going out for a walk, mom."

"Please think about how good it will be after

quarantine," she said hopefully, as she watched Billy and Henry walk out the front door.

They started walking their usual route, Henry chasing jackrabbits here and there, disappearing over the rim of a canyon, then giving his one bark of frustration before returning to Billy. His mind was preoccupied by the unfairness of the situation. His mom falling in love, and Henry having to go into quarantine. He was torn between the right thing to do; please his mom or be selfish. He kept coming up with alternatives, asking himself questions to ameliorate the situation. We don't have to go, but mom wants to go. Why doesn't Steve get a job in a state that doesn't have quarantine? There's plenty of hospitals in America, why Hawaii? Mom deserves to be happy. This might be her last chance to find someone she loves. She's not getting any younger. I can't let her down after all she's done for me, but six months for poor Henry in a cage and kennel.

While Billy was pondering all these scenarios in his head, they started walking higher into the mountains, reaching the beginning of the pine forest. Although the beginning of May, patches of snow still littered the ground. While Billy kept wrestling with this problem in his head, please his mother, commit Henry to six months quarantine, tell Steve to get a job in the mainland, if he really loves her, he'd do that etc., he wasn't paying attention to the trail that all but disappeared. With all these thoughts racing in his head he stepped on a patch of snow with no ground underneath it. It was a hollow and he fell tumbling and bouncing fifty yards down a steep ravine. All he saw was a rush of sky, trees and ground as he tumbled to the bottom.

When he finally came to a stop on his back, a hot searing pain shot from the shin of his right leg. Fighting back the intense pain, he tried touching his shin, the source of the pain, only to be shocked to feel bone sticking out from where the pain was emanating. Soon he saw that part of his jeans where his shin was broken started turning red and damp with blood. The area around it started swelling up to the size of a grapefruit. Every time he tried touching his leg to assess his injury, the pain caused him to flinch back. Henry finally got down the ravine and started licking his face.

"I'm okay, boy. It's okay, boy," he said to Henry calmly, trying to reassure him. He tried standing up, but the pain was so intense he laid back down. After a few more tries, he knew it was useless. He was stuck here and knew the only way out was to get help. He saw his backpack a few yards from him, but too far to reach.

"Get the pack, boy. Get the pack," he told Henry, pointing to the backpack. They played this game at home. He'd tell Henry to get a toy from his toybox, and Henry would always go and choose a toy to play tug-of-war and bring it to him. Henry looked at him, unsure of the command or what Billy wanted him to do.

"The pack, boy, GET THE PACK!" said Billy again, pointing at the backpack. This time Henry knew what to do and walked over, picked the pack up in his mouth, and brought it to Billy.

"GOOD BOY, good boy!" said Billy praising him. He opened the flap where he kept his phone and dialed home. No response. No signal. They were out of reach. Billy started stressing about how they were going to get help and get out of here. Billy dialed again. No response. No signal. Mom will start worrying when we don't get home for dinner, he thought, and come looking for us.

Billy took out the apple and shared it with Henry. After eating their apple he gave Henry some water, taking a few sips himself and they only drank half, as he thought it might take his mom more than a day to find them. The granola bar he'd save for tomorrow as it looked like they were going to spend the night in the woods. The temperature began to drop. The pain in his leg eased into a dull throbbing ache, and he started feeling feverish. He tried getting up one last time but it was useless. He made himself as comfortable as possible on the hard ground. Henry came over and lay next to him providing some warmth for the cold night. There were no thoughts of Hawaii as he fell into a numb feverish sleep.

"Steve, it's eight o'clock and Billy and Henry aren't home yet," said his mom over her phone.

"Did you tell him about Hawaii and quarantine?" he asked.

"Yes."

"How'd he take it? Especially about Henry?"

"Not good, but this isn't like him."

"Maybe he's out still mulling it over. He's a responsible boy. I'm sure he'll be home soon."

"I feel like I should call the police."

"Wait another hour, that's when I finish my shift and be home. It'll be okay, he's a good boy. I love you." And hung up.

When Steve got home and still with no sign of Billy, his mom called the police. They told her he couldn't be reported missing until after twenty-four hours and call them back. She tried convincing them but to no avail. She gave them a description of Billy and what he was wearing. She told them he had his dog with him, an Airedale. The cop looked up Airedales on his computer and said, "So that's what an Airedale looks like." She also told them about their conversation about possibly moving to Hawaii, quarantine for Henry and how upset he was. The cop told her the same thing Steve had said, that he's probably still thinking it over and he'll be home soon. When she hung up Steve was no longer so sure. Her mother's instinct telling her something was not right. She knew her son better than anyone.

Billy woke up to the sound of birds chirping and wan sunlight filtering through the trees. If it wasn't for the pain in his leg, he would've thought he was on a camping trip. Henry was snuggled next to him, keeping him warm during the cold night. He was surprised to see puffs of clouds coming out of his mouth each time he exhaled. Henry got up and stretched. Billy was stiff and sore and tried to move, but a searing pain shot into his sleepy brain forcing him to stop. He leaned over, unzipped his pants, and relieved himself. The smell of his urine only inches away. The smell of the homeless he thought. Henry walked a few yards away and did his business. He returned to Billy and started licking his face, encouraging him to stand up. Billy tried, but it was useless. He sat back and looked at his watch, seven o'clock.

"They'll be here soon, boy," he told Henry. "It'll be all right, we'll be home soon." And buried his face in Henry's neck. Although he was feeling miserable with fever and pain, he knew his mother would rescue them.

Early next morning, Billy's mom and Steve went to the

police station. They both pleaded with the police to go and search for him. Being a doctor and nurse, respected members of the community and after much convincing, the police decided not to wait the full twenty-four hours and agreed to look for Billy. His mother giving them information on the trails they usually took and their local dog park. Two police officers were sent to look for Billy, Steve and his mom went to the main trail.

While police interviewed people at the dog park, showing them photos of Billy and Henry, his mom gave them, she and Steve started on the main trail. There was no one to be seen for miles around on this crisp cool morning. When they started reaching higher ground they began yelling, "Billy, Henry, Billy, Henry," at the top of their lungs.

"Do you think they would've gone this far?" asked Steve.

"He wasn't allowed, but he was so upset about losing Henry for six months."

"Do you think he ran away from home?"

"Don't be ridiculous. He'd never do that. Are you gonna help me find him or not," she responded angrily. Peeved off at such a suggestion about her son.

Trekking higher, they started yelling again, "Billy, Henry, Billy, Henry," continuing up the mountains, stopping now and then to follow other trails, making sure they weren't missing any signs of them before returning to the main trail. It was time consuming, taking them most of the day, and with still no signs of Billy and Henry.

It wasn't until late afternoon when the two officers caught up with them. Telling them the people they interviewed didn't see them yesterday, and that they searched the trails around the dog park with no luck, and with calls to the station to see if they turned up.

"I'm sorry ma'am," said the young female officer, "nothing's turned up."

Billy's mom thankful for their help and thinking she only looked a few years older than her son.

It was getting dark, and they didn't have flashlights. Billy's mom wanted to continue searching and had to be convinced by Steve and the officers that it was too dangerous walking in this terrain in the dark. The police reassuring her they'd start again first thing in the morning and might even get permission for a chopper to help them in the search. It was only after hearing about the chopper did she agree to end the day's search. The thought of her son having to spend another cold night in the wilderness didn't sit well with her.

Billy gave Henry half of his granola bar. They then drank the rest of their water. It was getting dark again and the pain and fever were taking its toll on him. As the cold and darkness enveloped them, he started going in and out of consciousness in his febrile state. It was pitch black when he woke to Henry growling. Opening his eyes he thought he was in a dream. He saw a myriad of yellow lights shining at him. "We're gonna be saved, boy," he told Henry, thinking the yellow lights were flashlights coming to the rescue, but the yellow lights started growling. His heart dropped. Coyotes, he thought, and many of them. Drawn by the scent of his blood and injury. Every now and then Henry would charge at them baring his fangs and barking ferociously, forcing them to retreat. But every time he did this they retreated less and less away, surrounding them. Billy took out his phone and put the flashlight on, hoping the light would scare them away, and it worked until the battery died. But it also had the opposite effect on him, as he could see how many hungry and snarling coyotes surrounded them and felt helpless. He picked up two large stones before his light went out. It took him all the strength he could muster to stay alert while fighting the fever and pain. In his mind he kept hearing Mr. Sun yelling "fight, fight, fight!" Determined to fight them off. It was then that the pack attacked and he heard the God-awful sound of animals in mortal combat.

"Henry, Henry," he yelled before losing consciousness.

"Chopper one here. We're climbing to 5000 feet. You said this is where the search party ended yesterday?"

"Roger to that."

"We'll make circular motions at 5.5 then 6, then 6000 feet. Visibility good, we'll find them."

"Chopper one here. I'm at 6,500 feet. I've found him. He's in a ravine with a lot of carnage around him. Looks like dead coyotes and maybe dogs lying around him. Not a pretty sight. There's enough room to winch down a stretcher and fly him to the hospital.

"Good work chopper one. His mother will be relieved."

"Roger to that, and out."

CHAPTER 15

Billy woke up as if in a dream. Surreal. Looking at his surroundings all he saw was white. White ceiling. White walls. Everything bathed in white. He didn't know how he got there. Hospital he thought. The pain in his leg was gone. It took him a minute or so to realize his mother and Steve were at his bedside. It was then his mind snapped to reality.

"Where's Henry?" he asked loudly.

"Oh my dear, my dear," responded his mother, kissing him all over his face.

"Henry. Where's Henry, mom?" he demanded urgently, raising his voice and leaning up on his elbows.

"I'm so sorry Billy, but Henry didn't make it. He died protecting you."

"Noooo," came a mournful cry from deep within the recesses of his soul. It was a sound she knew all too well. The mournful wail that comes when told of the profound loss of someone you love dearly, love more than life itself. That plaintive wail of grief as it shatters your very being. It was the same cry that came out of her mouth when two army officers knocked on her door, telling her Billy's father died in combat. It was the same mournful wail that came out of her mouth at the airbase when he returned home in a coffin draped with an American flag, the sight causing her knees to buckle as she lay sobbing on the ground. And it was the same cry a week later, when his coffin was lowered into the ground, Billy barely two, clutching her leg. Only this time that sound was coming from her young son.

"No, no, this can't be true, he can't be dead, it's not true," he yelled, crying hysterically, tears flowing freely down his face. His yelling caught the attention of some nurses who rushed in to help. His mother knew one of them and nodded, signaling she had the situation under control. Her son was grieving the loss of Henry. She knew what to do.

She let him cry for a good ten minutes, saying "Let it out, let it out, let that pain out." Holding him in her arms, while Steve handed her tissues to dry his eyes and nose. When the crying turned to sobbing, she knew it was time to tell him.

"When the rescuers got down to the ground from the chopper, they found three dead coyotes near you, and Henry badly injured lying on top of you. He was badly hurt. It must have been awful. He was barely alive, and they winched both of you up in the chopper, but poor Henry died on the way to the hospital. He died saving your life.

Billy heard his mother's words, but they weren't registering. He was in shock. The first stage of grief. The emotion that protects humans from the pain of the profound and devastating loss of a loved one. Billy was feeling the pain from a wound so deep in his soul, that it made the excruciating pain from his shattered leg seem trivial. All that was good in his life had gone. Without Henry his life lost meaning. He wanted to curl up in a ball and die.

"It's my fault he's dead, it's my fault," he began wailing and crying again. His mother knowing grief all too well from experience just let him cry in her arms, knowing nothing she said would take his pain away. She knew his grief would eventually pass. It may take him years, she thought, like me, but the one thing she knew for certain was that only love lasts forever, and that Billy would love Henry for the rest of his life.

Eight days later Billy was released from the hospital. He suffered a complex fracture of his right shin, and the doctors had to reset his leg and place him in a cast from the knee down. They told him the operation went well, and when the cast comes off he'd have to do physical therapy for a few months until his right leg got stronger. He was also told the break wouldn't affect the growth of his leg. He was young and strong and would be fine to travel to Hawaii in the Fall. For now he'd have to use a walker to get around.

On the car ride home with his mom and Steve, he was quiet. Stoic. Happy to finally leave the hospital. Using his walker, he slowly walked up the path to their front door. When his mother opened it to let him in, he saw Henry's leash hanging on its' hook. The sight of it causing him to crumble to the ground in a burst of tears, knowing that he'll never have a walk with Henry again. Never spend another moment with the dog he loved more than anything in the world. His mother let him lie on the ground, sobbing helplessly until this wave of grief passed. After a few minutes, she and Steve helped him up and led him to the sofa to sit down. She waited a few more minutes for the sobbing to stop and the tears to dry. That's when she gave him a tuft of Henry's fur, she cut it off before she had his body cremated. She didn't want her son to see what the coyotes had done to Henry's body, and placed his ashes in an ornamental bowl, putting it on his lap. This caused Billy to start crying again. Billy clutched the tuft of Henry's precious fur in his hand and caressed his cheek with it sobbing, "Henry, oh Henry how I miss you, boy," over and over and over. Just like Jake in World War I his mother thought; Henry also deserved a medal for saving her son's life.

Henry didn't get a medal for saving Billy's life, he got something else, posthumous fame. A local reporter covering the local news got a tip from one of the chopper pilots about Billy's rescue and wrote in their city paper "Dog Saves Life of Boy from Coyotes in Mountain."

The story went statewide, then went national. The public was hungry for their story, and Billy was even flown to Los Angeles to be interviewed on morning television. Letters came pouring in from all over the country to the hospital who forwarded them to Billy's address.

The letters were filled with stories of encouragement, compassion and awe at how Henry had saved his life. Some spoke of the grief they experienced at the loss of a favorite dog, assuring him the pain from Henry's loss will subside with time. Many wrote the old adage that time heals all wounds to comfort him. Billy's leg healed, but his heart didn't. Although he appreciated all their words of kindness, he was left feeling empty. Mornings were the worst. When Henry was alive, he greeted him every morning with what Billy called his Stoochie dance. Approaching him with his head bowed low and tail wagging before licking his face. Henry's happy anticipation of the new day's adventure every morning filled his heart with joy. Now there was nothing but a painful void. Empty, like the middle of an onion. This was the time of day he cried the most.

Sometimes wailing in pain so loud it would wake his mother who would come rushing into his bedroom to console him. The sight of Henry's belongings made him cry. His bowl, his leash, his toys, spots on their morning walks where they'd stop and share an apple, a drink of water, caused the tears to come rushing out. There was one special spot on top of a ridge which gave a panoramic view of the desert before ascending to the mountains that caused him to cry the most. Billy called it Henry's spot because Henry would always stop and slowly survey the valley, looking for the movement of a jackrabbit. Billy would always drape an arm around Henry's body and ask, "Whatta ya see boy? Any rabbits?"

With a stick Billy drew a big H on the ground near a bush where Henry stopped and looked. It was here Henry's memory was strongest. Every time he passed Henry's spot, Billy would get down on his knees and say, "Henry, King of the canyons, may your spirit roam these canyons forever," and cry his heart out.

Billy went through his daily routines like a robot. He got all A's on his report card. He got his blackbelt from Mr. Sun. He continued jogging in the canyons and working out. He bought a locket and put the tuft of Henry's fur in it and wore it on a chain around his neck, giving him comfort to have a piece of Henry on his body.

Billy read about Rainbow Bridge. The heaven for the departed dogs of their human owners. A big grassy meadow where all the dogs would run around, have fun, playing and chasing each other. Every now and then a dog would stop playing and look at the bridge connecting it to the meadow and see a human crossing it. Although the human form would be fuzzy at first, the dog would know in an instant it was their owner and run at full speed to the bridge to be reunited with the person they loved the most. Although raised a Catholic, this was Billy's idea of heaven.

In the Fall, Billy, his mom, and Steve flew to Hawaii to start their new life. Henry's ashes went with them.

TWENTY YEARS LATER

"Doctor Martinez, emergency arriving in ten minutes, please go to the OR," came the announcement over the loudspeaker.

"I have to go now, I know it's not easy, but make sure Bailey gets a drop in each eye twice a day. Once in the morning, and once at night. Her eye infection should clear up in a few days. Call me if it doesn't get better in three days," he said, handing the lady the eye drops and giving Bailey a scratch under her chin.

"I've gotta go."

"Thanks doctor," replied Bailey's owner.

Dr. Martinez walked briskly down the hallway and into the emergency room. Washing and scrubbing his hands thoroughly, he asked the vet nurse what were they expecting.

"A boy and his mother called. Their dog threw up twice today, all his kibble and grass. He's never done that before, they're concerned there might be some blockage in his gut."

"Okay, we'll need to sedate him and get an X-ray to see what's happening down there."

Just then, the doors flew open, and two assistants carried his patient into the ER. He was surprised to see his patient was a full grown Airedale, as he didn't see that many Airedales anymore, having grown out of fashion to all the new doodle breeds. It reminded him of Henry.

"Here he is doc, the owners are in the waiting room, a young boy and his mom. They want to wait to see what can be done. Here's the signed insurance papers," said the assistant, handing him the paperwork.

Dr. Martinez scratched his patient under his chin while the nurse shaved the fur off one leg to prepare the intravenous.

"Don't worry boy, I'm gonna take great care of you, you're in good hands," as they adjusted the X-Ray machine over his body.

About forty-five minutes later, Dr. Martinez walked into the waiting room to find the boy and his mother seated in a corner.

"Hi, I'm doctor Billy Martinez," he said approaching them. "Archie's gonna be fine. We found a piece of corn husk lodged in his duodenum and took it out. You did the right thing bringing him here right away as time is of the essence. In these situations the blockage stops the flow of blood to the intestines and death is imminent, five or six hours at the most. We'll keep Archie under observation overnight, and if all is well, you can pick him up tomorrow.

"We'll give you a call. He'll be sore for a few days and have to wear a cone so he doesn't lick his stitches. I'll give you a course of antibiotics to give him for the next ten days. The stitches are the ones that are absorbed by the body, so he doesn't need to come back for me to take them out unless there's a problem."

The boy and his mother both gave a big sigh of relief, thanking Billy profusely for saving Archie's life.

"I don't know what we'd do if we lost him," said his mother. "Kyle loves that dog more than anything. He spends every minute of the day, except for when he's in school, with Archie.”

“Thanks doc,” said Kyle shyly. “He’s my best friend and I love him so much, I can’t even think about…” and started to cry.

“It’s all right, let it out, let it out, don’t be ashamed to cry,” said Billy, putting an arm around Kyle’s shoulder. “He’s gonna be just fine, and the two of you will be together soon. They’re great dogs Airedales. I had one too when I was your age.”

“Really?” said Kyle, wiping the tears with his sleeve.

“I sure did. His name was Henry, and he saved my life.”

“No way!” exclaimed Kyle with interest. “How?”

At this point a vet nurse approached them and said, “Dr. Martinez, your next patient is ready.”

Turning around to face her, he said, “Just give me a few more minutes, tell them I just finished an emergency,” and turned back to Kyle who was eager to hear about Henry.

“It’s kind of a long story, but when I was about your age, my mom promised to buy me an Airedale pup on my twelfth birthday if I got good grades for a year and did all my chores. I wanted an Airedale after reading about Jake in WW I.”

“Me too!” exclaimed Kyle. “He got the Victoria Cross for bravery.”

“That’s right. So I got my pup and named him Henry. He was the greatest friend and birthday present I got. We spent all our time together walking in the canyons, and he loved chasing…”

There’s an old saying about grief. That there finally comes a time when the thoughts and memories of a lost loved one bring a smile to one’s face before the tears. That time had finally come for Billy.

EPILOGUE (FIFTY YEARS LATER)

Billy lived a good long life. His reputation and compassion for dogs and animals in general made his veterinary practice grow so much that he opened another clinic on the other end of town. That one grew as well and over the next ten years he opened up two more veterinary hospitals covering all four corners of the city. He loved his work and never euthanized a dog or cat that didn't need to be put out of their suffering. That was the golden rule of his practices. Unwanted dogs or cats were adopted or trained as service or companion animals. Those who weren't adopted or trained to be companion or service dogs were placed on a five-acre farm be opened upstate in the country, where they would live their lives in comfort, running, chasing, and playing with each other. This was his legacy to Henry. He spent all his time working, doing research, writing papers, giving lectures, and saving the lives of thousands of dogs and cats. He didn't have time to get married until he was in his mid-forties. By that time, he employed a dozen vets, forty staff, and twenty vet nurses, one of whom he married. Her name was Judy, a farm girl from Oregon. They had two children, a boy Nicholas, who followed in Billy's footsteps and became a vet; and a daughter Olivia, who got an MBA and ran the business side of his four practices. He was blessed with four grandchildren, two from each child.

Billy worked religiously until he was seventy-five

loving what he was doing until prostate cancer slowed him down. He beat his cancer for ten years, getting to enjoy spending more time with his wife, kids, and grandkids. He spared no expense, taking them all on family trips to Europe, Africa, Asia and Australia until the cancer returned and spread to his bones.

Billy was a member of death with dignity, and his state allowed physician assisted euthanasia. While on his bed at home, surrounded by his family, his doctor asked, "Are you ready, Billy?"

"Ready as I'll ever be," he replied. "You know, I've ended the suffering of so many dogs and cats in my lifetime. It was something I never liked doing, but looking in their eyes, seeing the pain they were in, and the pain on the faces of their owners, I always knew deep down in my heart of hearts I was doing the right thing."

Turning to his wife, children, and grandchildren, he told them how much he loved them, and to always be kind to animals and live their lives to the fullest. Having said their goodbyes, they placed their hands on his body, sobbing.

"You know how this works Billy," said his doctor, "the first injection will make you woozy, the second will kill any pain, and the third will send you into a deep and final sleep."

"I'm ready," said Billy, clutching the locket he wore around his neck with Henry's ashes in his right hand. The doctor administered the first injection, as Billy smiled lovingly at his family. He knew this was the right time to leave this life and didn't want any more chemo and pain killers to make him linger on in a hospice giving up quality of life for quantity. He wasn't a religious man. He didn't believe in God or the Devil, but when his mother passed away, acknowledged that her Catholic faith and belief in God helped her through her final hours. Billy believed in Nature and Mother Earth, the cycles of life.

The doctor administered the second injection and heard his youngest granddaughter yell, "Don't go yet Grandpa, tell us another story." And started crying.

Billy looked at her and smiled. His mind wandered to a book he read about Zen Buddhism. They believed you die three times. First, when your heart stops beating. Second, when you are buried or cremated. Third, the last time someone says your name. Billy liked the last one as it was open to interpretation and debate. Billy's interpretation was that it finally opened the door for one to leave this life and travel on to the next, the final journey. The doctor administered the third injection, and the last word his family heard him speaking was,

"Henry."

Billy died peacefully with a smile on his face.

LIMBO AND PARADISE FOUND

Henry woke up and raised his head from a deep sleep. Pointing his snout up, he sniffed the air for the scents of any new arrivals. He was under the shade of a green leafy tree atop a gently rolling hill. The sun was shining so he squinted his sleepy eyes to adjust and focus on the scene below. From his vantage point, he could see the whole of the big, green, grassy meadow below. It was full of dogs playing with each other as far as his eyes could see. Every breed imaginable was there, from majestic Great Danes to the tiniest of Chihuahuas, mixed breeds and mutts were all running, chasing, play-fighting with each other just like in a dog park. Except here, there were no fences or humans, no fights or aggression, it was all fun and play. There were no sick, old, or maimed dogs. They were all healthy, just like him, in the prime of their lives.

He got up on all fours and gave himself a good downward dog stretch and turned his head to look at the stream below, slowly meandering its' way to the big lake where he could see all the Labradors and other water dogs splashing each other as they raced along the shoreline playing chase. Some were jumping on each other's backs while others were swimming towards a small island in the middle of the lake. The island was surrounded by a sandy white beach where the dogs shook the water off their coats before frolicking with others on the shore. The middle of the island was full of leafy trees providing shade and rest after their play.

Henry thought about walking down to the stream for a drink of its' cool fresh water but wasn't really thirsty. In fact, since he got to this place, he was never hungry either. Or cold, or sore, or sick. All his basic needs were provided. If he was hungry, his favorite meal of a bowl of kibble mixed with pieces of roast chicken would appear. Thirsty, he'd walk down to the stream for a drink. When he wanted, which was often, he'd think of a big jackrabbit to chase and suddenly, out of nowhere, one would appear, daring him to try and catch him. Henry would crouch down on all fours, belly scraping the grass, to sneak up on the rabbit, inching closer and closer when boom! The rabbit would shoot off like a rocket and the chase was on; Henry yelping with delight. After gaining ground and getting closer and closer to the rabbit, it would suddenly disappear into thin air, Henry giving one of his barks of frustration. The only thing missing from this place was his boy.

He didn't know how he got to this place or how long he'd been here. He just knew he had to wait. Limbo. A dog's life is spent waiting. They wait for their humans to come home from work, school, shops, the doctor, etc. and it isn't until that door opens, or they see them through the window, that all that is good in life becomes complete as they bark with joy, tails wagging to greet their owners at the door. The most important part of a dog's life is being together with their humans.

He remembered coyotes surrounding him and his boy in the woods. His boy was hurt and couldn't walk. It was dark, but he could smell the scent of hungry wild animals meaning to do them harm. He covered Billy with his body, shielding him as best he could as his purpose was to love and protect Billy with all his life. Lunging out and snarling at them from time to time, managed to keep them at bay. Henry had no fear and remembered the anger welling up in the pit of his gut at these wild dog- like animals who wanted to hurt his boy. The ferocity that overtook him when they attacked after Billy's light went out.

In the darkness, a figure came flying at them, but Henry was quicker, grabbing the coyote by the throat and throwing him over Billy. Immediately, another attacked, and Henry was able to throw it on its' back and sink his fangs into its' belly. The warm blood putting him in a fighting frenzy as he grabbed another one by the neck, shaking it vigorously from side to side with his powerful neck muscles. As he was doing this, he felt fangs grabbing him from behind, pulling him off Billy. He reached behind to fight off his attackers and then he was here.

Henry glanced at the bridge, connecting the grassy meadow with the other side of the stream. The other side obscured by thick white clouds. The bridge was a simple wooden structure, a small foot-bridge. From time to time he would see a dog stop playing and run to the human crossing it from the cloud side to be reunited with the human they loved. This happened not too long ago with his puppy friend Tucker. Henry missed Tucker, but there were other dogs to play with and rabbits to chase when suddenly a big jackrabbit appeared seemingly smiling at him, daring him to try and catch him. Henry snapped out of his reverie and the chase was on; Henry yelping with delight. The rabbit ran quickly down the hill and along the stream towards the bridge with Henry in hot pursuit. He was slowly gaining ground on it, almost within inches of finally catching one when it disappeared into thin air. Henry stopped and gave his bark of frustration when he caught sight of a familiar figure walking over the bridge. There was no mistaking who it was. His scent was unmistakable. Henry ran faster than he had ever run before. The wait was over. Billy wasn't an old man, he was just as Henry remembered and jumped on his boy yelping with joy. The tears flowing like rivers down Billy's cheeks. Henry stood on his hind legs, lapping Billy's tears from his face like water. Billy saying,

"Henry, Oh Henry, my boy, my boy, it's really you," crying with happiness.

"It's been a long long time, too long," said Billy, burying his face in Henry's coat, inhaling the scent he loved so much and never forgot. He was reunited with the dog that not only saved his life, but gave it meaning and purpose. The dog that made him devote his entire life to healing, saving, and recuing the lives of thousands of dogs and cats that came to his clinics. Wiping the tears from his face, Billy finally said,

"C'mon boy. Let's go for a walk."

Henry looked at him with those intelligent light brown eyes he missed all those years and led him to a trail that entered a thick pine cone forest with snow covered mountains in the far distance. Billy slowly began jogging up the trail; Henry stopping now and then, looking over his right shoulder to make sure Billy was keeping up. A smile crossed Billy's face as he remembered the most important lesson Henry taught him. *Every day can be an adventure*, and they disappeared together into the woods.

Printed in the USA
CPSIA information can be obtained
at www.ICGtesting.com
LVHW051512051224
798279LV00007B/36